Our
Cadaver

Our Cadaver

Elizabeth Toman

A Novella

Etchings Press
University of Indianapolis
Indianapolis, Indiana

This publication is made possible by funding provided by the Shaheen College of Arts and Sciences and the Department of English at the University of Indianapolis. Special thanks to the students who judged, edited, designed, and published this chapbook: Aaliyah Hughes and E. Alexander Phillips-Hedge.

UNIVERSITY *of*
INDIANAPOLIS

Published by Etchings Press
1400 E. Hanna Ave.
Indianapolis, Indiana 46227
All rights reserved

etchings.uindy.edu
www.uindy.edu/cas/english

Printed by IngramSpark

Published in the United States of America

ISBN 978-1-955521-30-7
27 26 25 24 23   1 2 3 4 5

Cover image by Cloudytronics
Cover design by E. Alexander Phillips-Hedge
Interior design by E. Alexander Phillips-Hedge

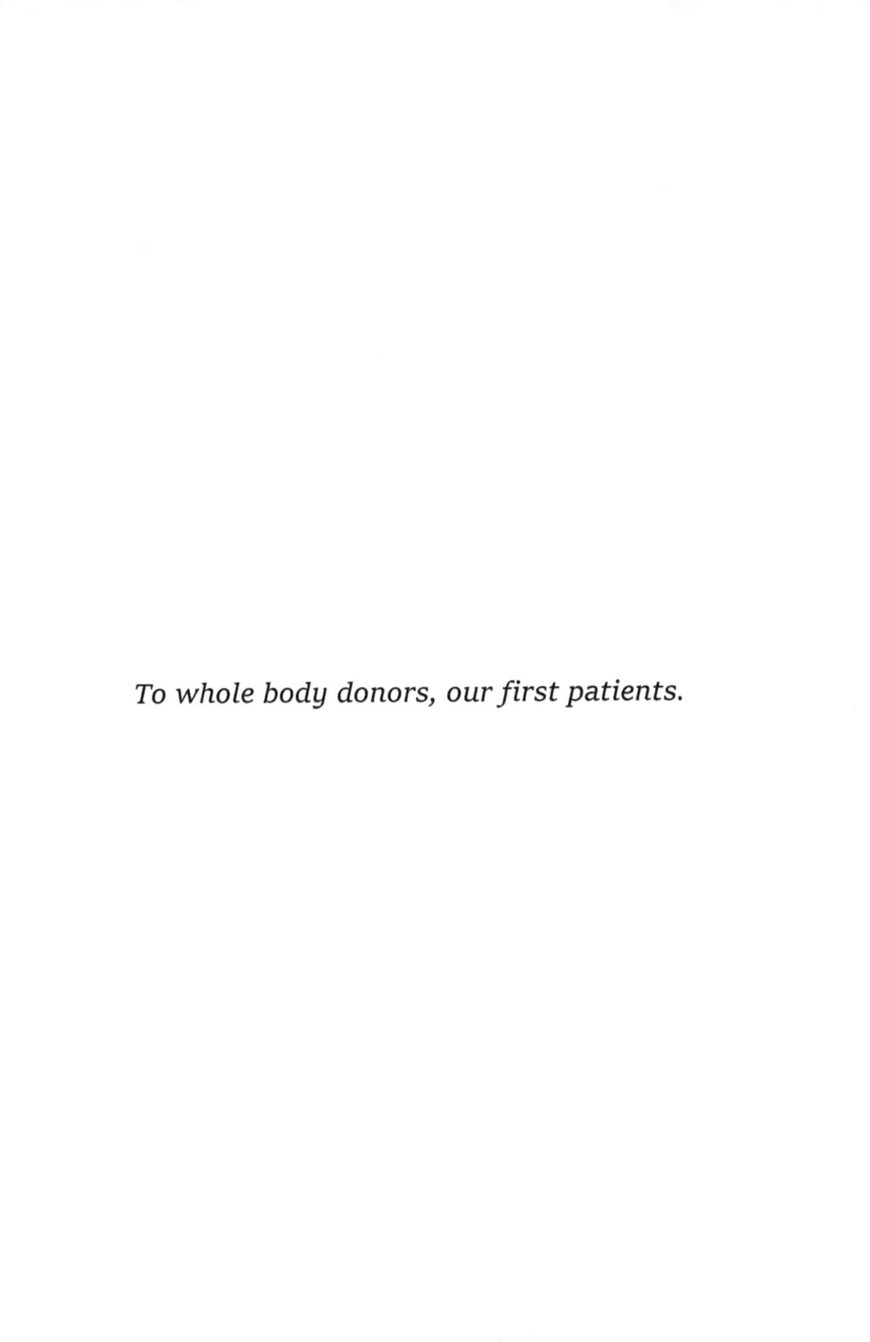

To whole body donors, our first patients.

I

Our cadaver was silent at first. He lay on the metal table like all the others, still and reeking of form-aldehyde. The odor would permeate my hair and skin the whole semester, regardless of the double layers of surgical gowns and the long, scalding showers that left me raw and sore that entire Chicago winter. Even today, I cannot smell formaldehyde without thinking of him.

Cadaver Lab B was a cavernous room and won-drously bright despite having only a single window in the far corner by the lab manager's desk. With its white walls, white linoleum floors, and row after row of fluorescent lighting on the ceiling, the effect was almost blinding when we first entered and saw our reflections on the chrome dissecting tables. Lat-er it would become a bustling and noisy place with the clang of dropped instruments and the chatter of students constantly in the background. That first day though, it was quiet as church. We stood erect and expectant around our assigned tables, clutching the plastic-encased tools we had been handed as we entered the room. The bodies were covered with dome-shaped steel lids that looked like chafing dishes at the buffet table of my college cafeteria, the fancy ones brought out for Parents' Day or other special occasions. When asked to spend a moment in silence before opening the lids to examine our cadavers, some of us bowed our heads. It looked like we were saying grace before a holiday meal, our implements ready to dig in.

Dr. Nash, our anatomy professor, paced among the tables as he lectured, his pointing stick grasped behind him. He seemed to be in his element and enjoying the tense attentiveness of the class that day. This was something he did not receive when standing at the podium in the lecture hall, where heads would nod and jerk awake at regular intervals and whispered conversations could be heard from the back. To keep us on our toes, he would look at the roster on his clipboard and call on students by name, asking questions he was sure they would not know the answer to. He would say, "You don't know? Folks, this was in the assigned reading." I had been called upon in this way on more than one occasion. He did not, I noticed, need to check his clipboard for my name. We were required to address him as Dr. Nash, unlike some of the other first-year professors, all of whom had PhDs rather than MDs and wanted to be called by their first names. On that first day of anatomy lab, he talked about the great sacrifice each of these individuals had made in giving their bodies to our university. He spoke of showing proper respect and decorum around our cadavers. "Think of them as your very first patient," he said.

Many of us had never seen a dead body before, and some of us had not seen a naked one other than our own. I had attended a few wakes by that time, but mainly remembered my mother laid out in her satin-lined coffin over a decade earlier. She had been carefully assembled in her best gabardine suit, her dark blue eye shadow and crimson lips just as she would have done them, sunlight streaming in from the window revealing a slight discoloration on her forehead where her head had hit the curb. In every dream I have had of her since then, she appears this way, lovely and unreachable, the bruise a sign of her demise. I discussed this quite a bit with the therapist they later sent me to because it was the most neutral topic we could come up with.

Our cadaver was a male, age 68, according to a toe tag which gave only his age and initials, J. B. He had leathery skin and coarse yellowish hair graying at the roots. We surveyed him from head to toe, trying not to linger too long on the genitals as Dr. Nash sauntered around the room, pointing out basic topography with his stick and lecturing on the importance of body habitus. I looked around and saw that all the cadavers lay supine, arms at their sides with palms upward, feet slightly parted. We all wondered, that first day, what kind of people they had been. What had made them agree to this? Some looked gaunt and chronically ill. Most were elderly. J.B.'s face was hard to read, with one eyelid barely open and his mouth agape. But I thought his expression looked kind.

At the next table, Stenger, a boy from downstate, gave a low soft whistle and whispered, "Ooh, baby!" as he inspected their cadaver. E.W., age 38, was an emaciated female, younger looking than most of the others, with single wisps of dark hair dotting her mainly bald head. Two of Stenger's lab partners chuckled uncomfortably, but the fourth, Stein, a tall woman from Evanston, squeezed the scalpel she had been issued until her knuckles turned pale. Stenger was rumored to have been responsible for the placement of Playboy centerfold images into Dr. Nash's slide carousel prior to a lecture on human topography. Many of our professors, when the same thing had happened to them, had found this funny, and half of the class laughed along. Dr. Nash stood stone-faced and, when he came upon the second image, told the class that if he found anyone tampering with his slides in the future, he would recommend expulsion. Expulsion! There were no more girlie slides after that.

Stenger also wore campaign-slogan tee shirts (*Let's make America great again,* and *Are you better off now than you were four years ago?*) all through September and October and handed out cigars after Reagan won in November. I gave him the benefit of the doubt about the slide show and forgave him his politics. He was from downstate, after all, and a product of his upbringing. But this blatant disrespect and humiliation of his cadaver were unforgivable.

My own lab partners stood rigid and disapproving. There were three others at my table, and I thought of them as "the Ws": Wilson, Weiss, and Welch. Wilson was the oldest, a quiet man, already married and with a master's in human anatomy. He was a brilliant student and had helped me once during the first semester with biochemistry problems. I was surprised when he told me he had applied to medical school three times before getting in.

"Why is that?" I asked. "I mean, you're such a great student."

He shrugged and said, "I got into a little trouble once when I was younger. This is my second chance, so I can't blow it."

I had gotten into a bit of trouble before myself during high school and then college. On top of that, my academic record was passable but not stellar. Still, I had not considered my admittance into medical school a second chance. I knew I would never have tried as hard as Wilson had, would never have pursued a master's degree in a related subject, and kept applying year after year. He wanted to be a surgeon, like his father, who worked at a small local hospital on the South Side, Lake Park, unconnected with any medical school.

Welch was charming and startlingly beautiful, with dark eyelashes and sharp blue eyes. I had often stared at him from my back-row seat in the semi-circular lecture hall and would need to break that habit now that he stood directly across from me. He grew up in Lake Forest, and someone had told me that his family was one of the wealthiest in Chicago, although you would never know it to talk to him. The rumor was that they disowned him when he was still in college. He'd had to delay admission for a year in order to work and was still up to his ears in debt. I couldn't imagine why a wealthy family wouldn't help their son through medical school or what they could have fallen out about. He seemed like the kindest, gentlest young man I had ever met.

Weiss was thick-set and studious, the hardest-working of any of us. He was always in the library, always early for lectures, and the one you could rely on for detailed notes if you overslept. That happened with some frequency in my case, and he got in the habit of routinely supplying me with Xerox copies of notes from the morning lectures in his neat block script. "Here you go, Zachry," he'd say with a feigned weariness. "Let me know if you need help understanding anything." Weiss was married as well, and his wife, a pale, soft-spoken woman, became known for delivering hot meals to him when we put in the long hours of our clinical years.

"Must be nice," Stein would one day comment to me, her voice dripping with sarcasm as we sat at a table in the closed cafeteria, eating cold bean sandwiches left for late-working residents and students. We were watching Weiss and his wife at another table, their heads tilted towards each other in intimate conversation while they ate steaming food from Tupperware containers. This was later, during our clinical rotations, and I thought, at the time, that it was nice. It was nice for Weiss to have decent food and love and companionship. It was nice that there was that little touch of humanity in our otherwise sterile institution. Weiss would end up in neurology and, years later, become my father's physician. As a doctor, Weiss could be dry and tedious, but he was also unfailingly thoughtful. I often thought that his wife bringing him those hot meals must have nourished that aspect of his personality.

All three of the Ws were superb students, but they were also genuinely guileless and kind, just the kind of people you would want to become doctors. Since I lacked those attributes, it made me wonder how I had been chosen. Was there another "W" out there, equally deserving, who had been denied a place in the class because of me? Instead of a Caroline Zachry, there would be a wholesome, ruddy-cheeked Wagner, hard-working and smart as a whip. Or rosy-cheeked, I suppose, since it would have been another woman: there were quotas in those days.

There had been a fifth partner assigned to us, Yee, who had not returned after the winter break. Someone had counted wrong in admissions as our class should have numbered one hundred twenty, a number divisible by four and perfect for the various labs and workshops we were assigned to. Instead, we were one hundred and twenty-one, and our end of the alphabet, the Ws, Yee, and myself, was always oversized. I had my suspicions about how this came to be and why I had been admitted. My father was a well-known oncologist at our hospital and had served as chief of staff for a number of years before stepping down when my mother became ill. I was hoping to keep this connection secret from my fellow students for as long as possible.

Everyone kept asking me where Yee had gone, assuming we were close friends because we were female and shared a microscope table in pathology lab. In truth, we spoke little, although it was not for lack of effort on my part. She was polite but did not socialize with her fellow students and seemed completely uninterested in anything to do with medicine. Instead of taking notes, she sketched or doodled during lectures, sometimes drawing elaborate designs that started with an anatomical representation related to the lecture and other times comical images of our professors or fellow students. She had chosen a seat just below mine in the lecture hall, a spacious oak-lined pit where we spent most of our first semester. We were often the only two students in that section, the rest of the class clustering nearer to the lectern. "Up here, and a little bit to the left, right Zachry?" she'd said to me one day as she sat down and retrieved a sketchbook from her backpack. I liked watching her drawings progress during class and found her almost as absorbing as Welch. Despite her seeming inattention, she received the highest marks, and her name was perpetually on the honor roll. I admired her immensely, as I did all confident women. In pathology lab, she allowed me more than my fair share of time with the microscope because she already knew the slides inside and out. Her father, it turned out, was a pathologist, and when I asked her if she was thinking of following in his footsteps, she raised her eyebrows and said, "That's the plan."

There was nothing unusual about going into the same specialty as one's father. It was almost the norm among students whose fathers were physicians, which must have been at least a quarter of the class. Stenger was destined to become an orthopedist, for example. Stein would go into cardiology, Wilson into colorectal surgery. Ophthalmologists begot ophthalmologists; urologists begot baby urologists. It was an age-old story. My father's friends, after suppressing their initial surprise that I would be attending medical school at all, always asked whether I would be following in his footsteps and becoming an oncologist. I didn't know, I would say, although I thought to myself that I could never enter a field as depressing, as full of death as that. I had no idea which specialty I wanted to pursue at that point. I only knew I wanted to become something different than what I had been. Someone more stable, more solid. Someone who did not take any drug offered to them or sleep with any boy who asked. Someone my father could be proud of.

When Yee did not show up that second semester, despite rumors of illness or mental breakdown, my first thought was that she had finally rebelled against her family and headed off on her own, perhaps to attend art school. That was my hope, anyway. I often wondered, though, if things would have turned out differently if she had been present those first few weeks of anatomy lab when we started dissecting J.B.

II

Dissection began on our second day of lab. The first day was all about naming external features of the human form. We had been studying anatomical terms for several months already, in lectures and from our textbooks. There had been a choice of two texts: Gray's, a thick tome with smaller illustrations, many in black and white, and lots of tiny text, and Clemente's, a more modern, atlas-style book with many full-color plates. Most of the class had chosen the former after Dr. Nash had referred to Clemente's as "more of a picture book" during a lecture. I later overheard him telling a small group of students that someone else in the department had insisted that Clemente's be an option purely as an appeal to novelty, to the fallacy of modern educational techniques being better, as though medical school required some sort of dumbing down. He was quite indignant. Gray's, he went on, was the gold standard and more appropriate for the serious student of anatomy. That clinched my decision to spring for the Clemente's, even though it cost half again as much as Gray's.

One day I was in the library sitting at my study carrel with Clemente's open to a full plate illustration of the dorsal foot. Yee walked by and stood over me for just a second.

"Another picture book fan, I see," she said, peering for a second over my shoulder. "You've got good taste, Zachry." I remember feeling delighted with that comment. I don't know why Yee's approval was so important to me.

We began with the lower leg. Weiss and I were positioned on the cadaver's right, and Wilson and Welch were on the left. Many of us felt some hesitation at making that first incision, and I was no different. To take a scalpel and plunge into the intact skin of a perfectly whole human form, however inanimate it may be, takes some courage, at least the first time you do it. Weiss, ever the eager beaver, volunteered to start on our side while Wilson, after a polite exchange with Welch where each insisted the other must do the honors, began on their side. Weiss made a mess of it, cutting too deep and severing the anterior tibialis tendon we were supposed to find. I was not much help to him. Although I did not think of myself as squeamish, I could barely watch those first few incisions, looking instead at the cadaver's face for signs of pain, although I knew that was absurd. I was averting my eyes as he hacked away, and the withered ends of the tendon shrank back into the spongy tissue before we could retrieve them with our forceps.

"Too bad," said Dr. Nash as he stopped by our table to look at our progress. "Mr. Wilson looks like he has it, though." We all watched as Wilson deftly peeled back the skin exposing the anterior compartment, then teased out the tendon, moving the muscle to the side and even freeing up the deep peroneal nerve. His movements were precise and graceful, his long forefinger probing the firmness of the tissue while his right hand picked delicately with the forceps. We might have learned the most just watching him, but he insisted that Welch have a turn after a while. He even came over to our side and managed to locate the distal end of the tendon for us, clamping it so we would not lose it again and demonstrating its action by tugging on it and causing the foot to dorsiflex. He was so much better at dissecting than anyone else in the lab that Dr. Nash would eventually recruit him as an unofficial teaching assistant.

It was the third week of class when I first noticed our cadaver, J.B., move. I was not sleeping much. My final first semester grades had returned and were astonishingly low. I had not been in the habit of working very hard at the small liberal arts college I had attended before medical school. I was accustomed to writing papers and answering essay questions that required long, thoughtful responses but not to memorization of page after page of information. I had been taught to think, not to memorize, I told myself, hearing the flimsiness of that excuse even as I made it. I was determined to succeed this second semester and was devoting long hours to studying, memorizing nerves, bones, muscles, and their insertions, quizzing myself, inventing new mnemonics.

We were starting on the upper limb, and Dr. Nash was prowling the room, his pointing stick flicking restlessly behind him. Welch and I were working on the right hand and had peeled away the dorsal skin when Nash stopped directly behind us and just stood there, not saying a word. He did this sometimes, just to frighten us, I thought, although he seemed to stand by our table more often than the others. I had noticed that he also liked to stare at Welch. He turned to me, pointed out a tendon on the periphery of our dissection field, and asked what it was. I could feel my lab partners tensing on my behalf. They leaned in closer, ready to rescue me from humiliation. "The polliscis abductus longus?" I asked, pretty sure of my answer but not wanting to seem overconfident.

"Origin and insertion?" he asked, and when I answered correctly, he nodded his head. "Very good, Zachry," he said as he walked away, motioning for Welch to follow. "You've been doing your reading, I see." My lab mates grinned, saying, "Way to go, Zachry!" As they returned to their work, I saw the right hand move very quickly. It formed a brief "thumbs up," perfectly demonstrating the action of the tendon I had just identified. The shiny tan surface went taut and then loose again through the open skin. It happened so rapidly that I thought I might have imagined it. But at the same time, I knew I had not. I stood dumbfounded and then looked at the others. Weiss and Wilson were busy with the left hand, and Welch had stepped away and was speaking with Dr. Nash in a corner of the room. Nobody looked as though they had seen anything unusual. I steadied myself, leaning on the edge of the dissecting table.

"Caroline? Are you okay?" Welch had returned and was looking at me with concern.

"Just cramps," I said. I had no idea why I said that. I was not the kind of young woman who invoked menstruation to avoid scrutiny or provide excuses. I'd never had cramps and thought of girls who complained of them as weaklings, but it was the first thing that came to my mind. Welch didn't flinch. He nodded sympathetically and asked if he could get me something.

"Some aspirin?" he asked. "If you want to go lie down in the lounge, I can cover for you." I shook my head. The cadaver's face was as immobile as ever, but for the briefest moment, I thought I saw a glimmer from the half-opened eye.

This was only the beginning. At first, the gestures always followed my doing something right. The second time it happened, I had just correctly identified the brachial nerve on the right side, preventing Weiss from cutting right through it. All four of us peered down into the upper arm as Wilson probed around to confirm what I was saying, but only I noticed the hand moving into the thumbs up position again. The third time was after Dr. Nash handed back a quiz on which I had received a perfect score, saying, "This is more like it, Zachry." I quickly covered the hand with my two hands, knowing what was going to happen this time. Once, while leaning over the body and helping to identify the radial artery on the opposite side, I felt the thumb rise and stiffen against my abdomen. I jumped back, startled, but said nothing. What could I possibly say?

In any case, the gestures felt private, meant only for me. The face would remain placid each time: a mask with no signs of life, the funny half-closed eyelid always in the same position. One afternoon, after Stenger had been particularly obnoxious, making rude comments about his cadaver, we all found J.B.'s third finger extended and pointing towards Stenger. The Ws accused Stenger, known for pranks, of doing this himself. Stenger shrugged and said, "Maybe he was trying to communicate with our gal here," referring to their cadaver. "She's gotta be one hot chick to an old geezer like that." Stein's face turned dark and mottled while I felt myself blanch. I had seen the finger uncurl itself and was certain that J.B. wanted to tell me something. Something more than "Way to go, Zachry."

When Stenger made offensive comments, Stein would usually scowl, and I would shake my head, but neither of us ever said a word to him. This time, though, it was Wilson who had had enough. He put down his scalpel and walked over to Stenger, smiling, and asked if they could talk. They stepped away from the tables to a far corner of the room, and I could see Wilson speaking, his head ducked down as he spoke in a quiet voice while Stenger shook his head petulantly, like a child who had been caught and refused to admit it. Wilson was extremely tall and often tilted his head down to converse. He was one of only a handful of African Americans in our class, several years older than most of us and considerably more dignified in manner. I remember overhearing the Dean of Students ask him, on the very first week of school, whether he had played basketball in college and the tense, tight little smile on Wilson's face as he shook his head. I'd caught the glint of anger in his eyes as the Dean walked on, and I tried to flash him a sympathetic smile as though I, too, were accustomed to being asked such stupid questions.

Our school was not known for diversity but there were a handful of African Americans, as well as a few Korean Americans, including Yee, two or three Chinese Americans, a woman from Vietnam who had come over during high school, a man from India, twin brothers from Puerto Rico, and a Palestinian-American woman. I remember all this because Stein took an informal census early on in that first year. She also made a point of counting the number of females in our class and several years of classes that preceded ours and discovered it always came out to exactly twenty-five percent, even though the school claimed to have dropped quotas. We tended to congregate at the end of the alphabet, both the women and the people of color, making me wonder whether the admissions committee reviewed applications alphabetically and felt the need to start scrambling when they got to the R's.

As I watched Wilson speak with Stenger I admired his measured approach all the more because I'd seen that same angry look in his eyes when Stenger made his remark. I would like to have eviscerated Stenger publicly, but lacked the courage or skill. I had the sense that Wilson was getting through. I was standing closest and heard the words "mother" and "sister" but could not make out exactly what was said. Dr. Nash went over after a while, noticing that we were all watching them, and asked, "Gentlemen? Is there a problem?" They both shook their heads, and I think Stenger was better after that. At least about his cadaver.

III

It was about that time that the lab opened up on Tuesday and Thursday evenings for optional study sessions, and I started attending regularly. I was determined to do well in the class and was devoting all my time to my studies. The first session was packed, with nearly the whole class turning up. The numbers started dwindling when my classmates realized that attendance would not be taken and Dr. Nash would not be there, only Bruno, the cadaver lab manager.

Bruno was an older man with a Czech accent and a single unruly gray eyebrow that rose and fell as he wandered through the lab peering over our work. When he thought we were doing a good job, he made little humming sounds, and his eyebrow rose almost up to his hairline. When we were not, he would issue a low grunt and the eyebrow would descend, bunching up over his nose. Sometimes, if we were stuck, he would even lean over to point us in the right direction using an old-fashioned trocar that dangled constantly from his finger, moving aside tissue to expose the elusive muscle or vessel we sought. He would hum even louder then, but we could not prevail upon him to explain to us what he saw. "That," he always told us, "is only for professor."

Bruno had managed the cadaver lab for years and was clearly not happy about these extra weeknights, an innovation for struggling students like me. He would sit at his desk, thumbing through papers, and occasionally crack the window to smoke a cigarette even though it was January, blowing the smoke through the opening and watching the lights of the hospital rooms across the street. At 8:30, he would start drumming his hands on his desk impatiently, then at 8:45, he would walk around the room briskly, saying, "Time to close them up, miss," or "Last round." He called the female students "miss" and the males "doc." You could see the men beam the first time he called them that, straightening up, taking their hands out of their pockets. It bothered some of the women, Stein included, and she went so far as to tell him once, "You know I'm also going to be a doc," to which he merely nodded and said, "I know, miss, I know." But I liked Bruno and did not care what he called me, especially because as the evening attendance thinned out, he did not mind giving me my space.

The first actual conversation I had with J.B. happened one night after Bruno left the room. He did this often, going out to grab a coffee or a snack at the hospital cafeteria, saying, "Mind the shop, would you, miss?" as he walked out. I was alone, as usual, the other students having packed it up after the first hour, and I was bent over the right foot, trying to work out the blood vessels, intent on my work. I heard a coughing sound from somewhere to my left and looked up quickly, thinking Bruno had returned already. But I was still alone. Thinking I had imagined it, I returned to the foot, but after a few seconds a voice, low and raspy, spoke from the head of the table.

"Got a smoke?"

I looked around again, praying that Bruno had returned, but I knew it was not Bruno. I had become accustomed by then to the hand gestures and was no longer frightened by them, but I was able to excuse them in my mind, to justify them as some sort of post-mortem reflex, perhaps something we had not studied yet. All the while, I knew that J.B. had been trying to communicate with me. Still, I did not dare to look at J.B.'s face. It was almost as though I had been waiting for this: on the one hand dreading and on the other hoping for it. I went on with my work, pretending I hadn't heard, until I glanced up and saw the thumb gesturing towards my backpack on the floor behind us and heard, "Hey Kiddo, how about it?"

"Kiddo" was something my mother used to call me before I turned into a defiant teen and asked her to stop. I had not been called that by anyone for years. I finally turned to the source of the voice, J.B.'s. head.

This time I saw the corner of his mouth open and saw that his left eye, the one that was usually closed, had also opened, just a slit. There was no mistaking that J.B. was staring right at me.

"You can't smoke in here," I whispered, afraid of being overheard. I was not certain if these rules applied to the dead as well as the living.

"Rusky there does it all the time," he said, gesturing with his lips towards Bruno's desk. "Come on, he won't be back for a while." The way he spoke so pleadingly from the side of his mouth, the left side still paralyzed, made me overcome my hesitation and take pity. I retrieved the pack of Marlboros at the bottom of my backpack, lighting one up and taking a long drag to get it going. I had no idea how he knew that I smoked, this being a secret I kept even more closely guarded than the identity of my father. I later came to think it was because he had so much time lying there to study us, our gestures and facial expressions, to observe the way we worked and interacted. His cold lips pursed and weakly grasped the cigarette as I held it to them. He managed a surprisingly deep inhalation and blew smoke out of his nose and mouth in a satisfied way, saying, "Jesus, that's good."

We smoked in silence for a while, sharing the cigarette. It would have felt rude to stop smoking it just because his lips had touched it. The formaldehyde taste was not so bad and grew weaker with each puff. Then I heard Bruno at the door, saying, "Time's up, miss," and I quickly snuffed out the cigarette on the floor and tidied my tools. "Thanks, Kiddo," he whispered as I lowered the lid over him. That was how our friendship began.

Over the next few weeks, we developed a ritual. I attended every evening session, and we would wait for Bruno to leave the lab for a break, as he always did, but I would continue working as though nothing was different. Then, J.B. would cough or clear his throat a few times and finally say, "Hey, how about a smoke break?" or "Are you gonna make me beg, Kiddo?" I would laugh and fetch the pack from my backpack, then move my stool up close to his head where we would share the cigarette and chat. We spoke whenever we could. I arrived early to every afternoon lab, often before anyone else, and we would have low, whispered conversations until my lab partners arrived. If Bruno or Dr. Nash were there, I would prop the Clemente's up close to the head so I could pretend to be studying or reading aloud if either one came near.

At first, it was mainly the smoking in the evenings, and some small talk. J.B. liked to hear all about my life, how my other classes were going, and what I did in the evenings I did not spend with him. The truth was that I did not do much. If there was no lab, I would stay at the library until closing, then trudge across the ice-encrusted parking lot to my dark apartment to study some more. I was terrified of failing but was having trouble focusing. The words would blur and jump in front of my eyes and my mind wandered constantly. On weekends I might visit my father at his home, my childhood home, in River Forest and drink tea with him in his study where every surface bore a photograph of my mother. There she was, beaming in her wedding dress, clutching me as a toddler, laughing as she threw a snowball. We would talk about my studies, pretending she was not there.

J.B. always asked about the weekend and then scolded me, saying, "That's no life for a young lady. You gotta get out there, see some action, Kiddo." I would shrug and say I'd seen plenty of action and just wanted to stay home now. He liked to talk about the Ws and the students at nearby tables and wanted to know all about their social lives. The first time he brought them up, it was clear he was hoping to set me up with one of them.

"How do you like Weiss?" he asked.

"I like him fine," I said.

"But do you like him?"

"He's married, you know."

"Just as well," he said. "He'd bore any woman to tears within five minutes." I had to laugh in agreement at that. Weiss was not scintillating company but he would become an excellent neurologist and help me tremendously after my father developed Parkinson's in his later years.

"Wilson seems like a good enough guy," he went on. "Too bad he's..."

"Already married?" I interrupted, worried he might be about to use some racist epithet. That would have been common enough for someone like J.B.

"Yeah," he said. "Too bad he's already married. He seems like the best of them." I was relieved by that statement, and we were both silent for a moment, thinking about Weiss and Wilson.

"Kiddo," he finally said, in the tone of a parent having a serious conversation with their teenager about the facts of life, "I can tell you like Pretty Boy." That's what he called Welch. "I've seen you looking at him." He paused, and I felt my face grow a little warm.

"But I wouldn't get my heart set on that guy."

It was true that I had a bit of a crush on Welch back then. He was so handsome and thoughtful, finding an anatomy illustration in Gray's and holding it up while the rest of us poked and prodded, holding the door open for everyone, asking how I was and sounding like he meant it. At the time, I denied having an interest in any of the Ws or anyone else in my class and said I wasn't there to find a man.

"Marrying a doctor is what most girls used to dream about," J.B. said to me.

"I'm going to be a doctor; I don't need to marry one," I told him.

"I know, but if you just married one, you wouldn't have to work so damned hard. You could let the fellow do it for you."

I asked him if he had any daughters, and he gave a little snort and said, "How about another smoke before Rusky gets back?" Rusky was his name for Bruno, although I had explained to him he was not Russian. There was a pattern in this. Whenever I tried to ask J.B. something about himself, he would quickly change the subject.

One day I was elected to open up the anterior thigh. I had been squeamish about using the scalpel, especially since becoming friends with J.B., but this time the Ws insisted I do the honors. My hand was shaking as I started slicing through the skin, and when I glanced up at J.B.'s face, he blinked ever so slightly, letting me know it was OK to go on. Later, after identifying the lateral cutaneous nerve, I saw his four fingertips extend, very briefly, the exposed tendons taut with exertion. I knew he was trying to give me a high five.

That night I asked him whether it hurt being dissected like that, and all he said was, "Kiddo, I can't feel a thing."

"But your nerves are all still there," I said. "Unless Weiss or I have cut them, that is." Weiss and I were way clumsier than our partners. We were clearly not destined to become surgeons.

"Well, there are nerves, and then there are feelings," J.B. said. "I find it's better not to spend too much time on either." Then he changed the topic.

IV

The day finally arrived when we were to open up the chests. Until then, we had been working mainly on limbs, sorting out the vessels, tendons, muscles, and nerves. We were looking forward to seeing what was "under the hood," as Dr. Nash put it. Weiss took charge of the procedure this time, and, as usual, his work was belabored and slow. It was excruciating to watch him cut through the skin and muscle and finally cleave the sternum. We grabbed either side with the rib separators and pulled with all our might until the lungs and mediastinum were revealed. I was shocked by the condition of J.B.'s lungs. They were dark and scarred, sodden with pink-tinged formaldehyde bubbling in the blebs and cysts that were everywhere. You could tell at once he had severe emphysema, and

I thought guiltily of the cigarettes I had been providing him. I snipped open the pericardium and could see immediately that his heart was a floppy mess. It was dilated and thin-walled and surrounded by fatty streaks, quite unlike the tight, pink fist of a muscle of E.W., the woman at the next table. Her lungs appeared pink and healthy on the outside, but we later discovered they were riddled with little tumors.

Dr. Nash stopped to look at our findings and observed that outward appearances could be deceiving. Our cadaver, he said of J.B., was an excellent example of what an unhealthy lifestyle of smoking and lack of exercise would produce. J.B. again extended his middle finger, this time towards Dr. Nash, and I had to discreetly fold it back into a natural position, patting his hand reassuringly.

That night was a lab night, and J.B. seemed morose, not his usual cheerful self. He kept complaining about what Dr. Nash had said, at one point saying, "I exercised every day of my life and I could pound that little faggot into the ground with one finger, alive or dead." I was worried he might attempt something when Dr. Nash came close, like grabbing a scalpel from one of us, even though he could really only move his lips and fingers. I tried to calm him down.

"You know how he is," I said in a low voice. "It's not personal." I lit up a cigarette and held it to his lips, but we found he could no longer smoke with his chest wall interrupted. It was too discouraging to watch him mouth the cigarette, smacking his lips like a fish out of water, the smoke just lingering there. I confessed that it was just as well, that I planned to quit anyway, not telling him that I had made that decision the instant I saw his lungs.

Normally this might have provoked a reaction from him, being a strong advocate of the benefits of tobacco, but instead he said, "How the hell did I end up here, anyway?" I thought he was talking about his death and tried to reassure him that it was not all his lifestyle, as Dr. Nash had implied.

"I don't know how much you remember," I said, "but it was most likely a heart attack, or maybe a stroke." I straightened up and launched into a little lecture. "There's genetics. You inherit tendencies to particular diseases, and there's not much you can do about that. You may or may not know what kind of health problems your parents had." I paused a moment, giving him the chance to tell me something about his parents, but he, as usual, declined to offer any personal information. "But whether you know or not, your parents' genes play a big role in what your own health will be like. Then there's lifestyle." I glanced regretfully at the cigarette butt I had not yet buried in the little Sucrets tin I kept in my backpack for that purpose. I went on to explain about smoking and cholesterol and fatty foods in my best fledgling doctor voice.

Although my classmates and I had yet to see a single living patient, we were endowed with a certain authority, an expectation of expertise, from the moment of our white coat ceremony that very first week of medical school. Strictly speaking, we had not earned it unless you count all that cramming for exams and brown-nosing of professors during our undergraduate years as somehow qualifying us to tell someone else something about their health. But we were all trying out that new voice, stretching our vocal cords to mew like newborn kittens, on non-medical friends and family when they asked us health questions, as they invariably did. We would develop a sense of authority that would grow steadily throughout our years of training, through medical school, residency, and fellowship if we took one. In some of us, it would reach a point of extreme arrogance somewhere in our late twenties or early thirties, until some incident, some dreadful mishap or mistake would reveal the unhappy reality that we were fallible, after all, and would wipe that supercilious look off of our faces. If we were lucky, it would not be a fatal mistake. J.B. cleared his throat, and I sensed I had lost my audience.

"You're gonna make a great doctor, Kiddo," he said. "I mean it. I wish you'd been there when I was so sick. Some of those guys, in their suits, their ballpoint pens scratching away, they never even look at you." He sighed. "But what I really meant was, how'd I end up here? At the goddamned med school. In this laboratory or whatever you call it, getting picked apart like a leftover Sunday chicken?"

I was mortified. Here I was, lecturing him on something he could no longer do anything about, and he hadn't even been talking about his cause of death. He went on.

"I left her a nice little nest egg and a life insurance policy. She couldn't be bothered to give me a decent burial?"

This surprised me. I had assumed, from what Dr. Nash told us, that all the cadavers were volunteers, altruists who had donated their spent bodies out of a true belief in doing good.

"Hell, no," J.B. said. "Who would volunteer for this? Do me a favor, Kiddo, go check on her, would you? See what she's up to." By "she," it turned out, he meant his wife of forty-three years, a woman named Marlene. There were no children, he told me. Some accident had rendered Marlene infertile before they met. I furrowed my brows, trying to imagine what that could mean. They had had a long and happy marriage, he said, and lots of friends. Marlene was the life of the party. Marlene was the love of his life.

I had not even known he was married. Our conversations were all about me, the opposite of the way it should have been since he was the patient. I was determined to make up for that.

The very next day, I sneaked into the lab and broke into the files by Bruno's desk as soon as I saw Bruno shuffling off for lunch. I took the precaution of opening up J.B.'s lid and propping up my Clemente's against his abdomen as though I was studying. J.B. watched me with interest from across the room. The cabinet was locked, but the key was sitting right on top. The cadaver files were organized by table number, and I located his within minutes. The first page contained his full name, Jerold Allen B., and basic demographic information like date of birth, date of death, and home address. I was interested to learn that J.B. had died over twelve months ago in our very own hospital, with the cause of death listed as cerebral vascular accident. A stroke! It was no wonder that he was fuzzy on the details. The next page held his medical history and I glanced over the list: coronary artery disease, congestive heart failure, diabetes, emphysema. There were no surprises there. The last document, "Consent for Anatomical Bequest," had several pages of legal jargon that I skimmed over quickly. The final page was the actual consent form with spaces for names and signatures. The form asked who was providing consent and there were two choices: "donor" or "next of kin." Sure enough, "next of kin" was circled followed by a name, "Marlene B., spouse," and then her signature. It was dated three days after his date of death.

I showed the document to J.B. and he twitched his lips in disbelief.

"How could she?" he asked.

"You never talked about this?" I asked, still finding it hard to believe that his body could have been donated without some sort of indication that it was what he wanted.

"Well, we joked around some times, about donating our organs. I said nobody would want mine. Christ, she knew I wanted to be buried near my folks in Woodlawn. We even looked into plots there once."

V

I went to see Marlene that same week, as soon as class was out on Friday, taking the Congress L and two buses to the Cicero address listed on the paperwork. I wanted to appear official but did not want to wear my own name badge, so after some contemplation, I took Yee's. She always left it dangling on the hook in our shared locker, and it was still there during winter term, clipped to the bright blue lanyard bearing our school's insignia and the words "primum non nocere" (first do no harm) over and over again. In retrospect, it seems stupid to have worn the name badge of someone who looked so completely unlike me. Yee was Korean and had dark, intense eyes that glowered from her ID photo. I, on the other hand, was fair-skinned and blue-eyed with a broad, bland look about me. It was a look that had allowed me to get away with all sorts of things in my wilder days, but would also cause patients to think me younger than I actually was over the next ten years of my clinical career. I hung the ID backward, as though carelessly put on, hoping the official-looking lanyard and appearance of some kind of badge would be enough to pass.

When I arrived at the house, a good hike from the bus stop, it was already getting dark, and the February air pierced right through the thin peacoat I had worn instead of my winter parka. I was hoping to look professional. The house was bleak, like the whole neighborhood, a tiny square structure with gray asphalt shingles, the front yard bare save for a single, scraggly shrub on the corner. I made my way up the icy path where soot-tinged snow had been piled unevenly on either side and was greeted by a rusted metal sign that read "no solicitors" at the bottom of the stairs. I paused for a second, pondering the meaning of the word "solicitor" before I ascended and rang the bell, halfway hoping no one would be home and I could turn around again, feeling I had at least tried. There was an enclosed porch and the stairs led immediately to its front door so you had to wait on a lower step. The door was opened right away by a woman I knew must be Marlene. She looked younger than I expected, although it was hard to tell with her heavy eye makeup and cascades of layered, artificially blond hair, in the style of Farrah Fawcett. She towered over me and narrowed her eyes.

"What is it?" she asked in a honeyed tone and

pointed to the sign. "You can't read?"

"Oh, hello," I said. My voice came out thinner than usual. I was shivering from both cold and nervousness but stood up straight and tried to sound competent. "I'm not selling anything. I'm a student from the medical school." She peered down at my official-looking clipboard to which I had attached the paperwork swiped from Bruno's files. "Are you Marlene B.?" I asked.

"What do you want?" she asked suspiciously.

I launched into my carefully rehearsed explanation, as she stared down at me from the two steps up. I was doing a survey, I explained, on behalf of the medical school. We are following up with bereaved families whose dearly departed made anatomical bequests. We wanted to know more about their decision-making process. Had she and Mr. B. discussed his donation prior to death, or did she learn of his wishes some other way? I did not lie outright as I spoke and tried to remain nonspecific. I was from the medical school, but "we" in this case referred only to J.B. and myself. Still, I found my face growing warm as I yammered on, Marlene eyeing me coolly. When I finished, she remained quiet for a moment, retrieving a cigarette from her housecoat pocket and lighting it with a hot pink lighter. She exhaled loudly, smoke clouding her face and making it appear worried.

"I've been over all that."

"I noticed that you were the one that signed the paperwork, not him. So I am assuming he put this in his will or put his wishes in writing in some other way?" I asked, trying to sound nonchalant.

"They told me they didn't need it in writing from him," she said, flicking her ash into the snow. "They were clear on that."

"Oh, alright," I said, talking too quickly, "I know we have cases where we accept whole body donations without the donor's written consent, but I just still need a little more information. Can you tell me when and where the conversation occurred?"

"Right after he died," she said. "I called the school right afterward."

"No, I mean the conversation between you and Mr. B., where he told you he wanted his body donated to the medical school," I clarified.

"Well, how in hell am I supposed to remember that?" she said, crushing the cigarette on the door jam and tossing it into the snow. "We talked about it all the time. 'Just donate me to science, honey,' he used to say, 'if I go first. Don't make a fuss.'" She said this almost mockingly in a low, raspy voice like J.B.'s. I had slowly inched my way onto the next step, try-ing to get out of the wind, and was hoping she might ask me inside. My fingers were going numb as I made a show of jotting notes onto my clipboard. Just at that moment, a male voice called out from inside the house through the cracked opening of the front door. "Honey, who's out there? You left the door open," and I saw a figure walk by the window. A man in boxer shorts and a t-shirt that clung to a pendulous belly paused at the inner door, a can of Schlitz in one hand and an oven mitt in the other. The warm odor of baking potatoes wafted out with him. Marlene ignored him and lit another cigarette.

"Look," she said, her voice sweet again. "It's what he wanted. They told me I didn't need any proof, that my signature would do. What makes you think he would have wanted anything else?"

"Well, we've had some irregularities," I started to say, pausing and then starting again. "There have been some concerns expressed."

"Concerns? By who?" Marlene asked, flicking her ash next to my foot.

"I'm not sure I am at liberty to tell you that," I said, sounding very unsure.

"Well, who can tell me, then?" she asked. "Because I'll tell you this is a hell of a thing, your coming here like this and bothering me after what I did for you. What we did for you. So I need to know exactly what the concerns are."

"Well, I believe it may have come from Mr. B. himself." Marlene gave me a questioning look. "Before he died," I said quickly. This was risky. I could pretend to have spoken with J.B. during his hospitalization, but I had not prepared for this line of questioning. I had not been expecting this level of scrutiny.

"That's crazy!" Marlene's laugh sounded like snorting. "He was a drooling idiot after that stroke. He couldn't say crap."

That was the moment my temper overtook my judgment. I knew she was lying and here she was, baking potatoes with a half-naked man while J.B. lay on that cold metal table. She had called him a drooling idiot. She had made fun of him.

"He told me himself," I said. "He would never have consented to it. He's miserable there and wanted me to come see you."

Her painted eyebrows shot up and her head tilted just a bit, but just then balloon-belly filled the outer doorway and said, "Now look here." I thought he was going to start arguing with me as well, but he was speaking to Marlene. "You're letting all the warm air out, baby. Invite the young lady in."

Marlene smiled, saying, "The young lady was just telling me she's been speaking with Jerry."

"Jerry who, baby?"

"My Jerry," Marlene said. "Our Jerry." The man looked incredulous and peered out at me.

"I think you misunderstood," I said, trying to backtrack and mumbling something again about J.B. having been in the hospital. Marlene interrupted.

"Now, do you remember where and when that conversation took place?" she asked. Her voice had turned sickeningly sweet. "The conversation with my deceased husband?" I opened my mouth to speak, but nothing came out.

"I think we're done here," she snarled and closed the door firmly in my face. It opened again almost immediately and she reached for my name tag, Yee's ID. I tried to jerk it away, but it was too late. She held it firmly and studied the picture, then narrowed her eyes and studied my face until I grabbed it back and turned around. "You didn't even bother to get a fake ID! You don't look like anything like that," she said as I stumbled down the stairs. "If you're really from the school, tell them they'll be hearing from me," she shouted after me.

I walked the long half-mile back to the bus stop, disheartened and freezing cold. When I reached my apartment nearly two hours later, I had to thaw out my feet in warm bath water before the feeling started to return. When it did, they burned like fire.

VI

I worried about Marlene's threat all weekend, hoping she would not follow through. I paced my apartment, tried to study, and brewed too many pots of tea. Monday, when anatomy class normally met, was President's Day, and school was closed. I met my dad for lunch after his hospital rounds in the special club reserved for medical staff and faculty where medical students were sometimes invited. I had avoided doing this before because I was worried about being seen with him by other students, the mystery of my acceptance to the school finally revealed. The place was nearly empty although he did manage to find one colleague to introduce me to. He looked so happy to be there with me, asking me about my classes, telling me about a difficult case he had as though we were working together. I smiled and pretended everything was going great, feeling guilty I had not met him there earlier.

On Tuesday, I was anxious and distracted all day, expecting someone to pull me aside any minute. I skipped the evening open lab session for the first time. I did not want to face J.B. with what I had learned about Marlene. Class met again on Wednesday but we could not speak with my lab partners present. I felt his eyes on me all throughout the session and sensed the questions behind them. *Had I gone? And?* I knew there would be no way to avoid discussing it. On Thursday, I had still heard nothing and started to relax a little. I trudged to the lab through the crusted snow, my breath crystallizing in front of me. I knew it was time to face J.B.

He was already awake when I opened the lid and immediately raised his eyebrow. I motioned with my head towards Bruno and two nearby lab tables where students were working. Things had been starting to pick up in the lab as midterms approached. When the other students left and Bruno took his break, we finally had our chance.

"So, what happened?" J.B. asked the second the door to the hallway clicked shut. "Did you go see her?"

"I did," I said, hesitating.

"She give you a hard time?" J.B. asked with that roguish half-grin. He seemed genuinely fond of her.

"She did," I said, sighing. I told him about the visit, how Marlene had stood at the top of the stairs looking skeptical while I pretended to conduct a survey. How she'd grabbed my pilfered name tag before I could get away. I described the man who was there, pleasant, balding, with a huge belly, but did not mention that he was in his underwear or that he called Marlene "baby."

"Oh, that sounds like my buddy, Pete." J.B. was thoughtful. "Glad he's looking in on her."

He asked how Marlene looked, what she was wearing, everything she said. I told him. He took it better than I thought, furrowing his brow when I told him what Marlene had said about giving his body to science. After a minute, he said, "Well, I don't remember anything like that. Maybe she just felt she needed the money. Still, she could have gone for cremation." We were silent for a few minutes while he contemplated this. I wondered how he could be so forgiving.

Finally, I said, "I thought she was serious about contacting the school. But I haven't heard anything. And no news is good news, right?"

"Oh, she'll call alright," J.B. said, smiling again. "There's nothing Marlene likes more than to make a stink. And the more wrong she is, the bigger stink she'll make."

"Oh," I said, my face dropping.

J.B. looked at me with concern. "Kiddo, you got nothing to worry about. Your dad can get you out of any trouble. Didn't you tell me he used to be a big shot here?"

"Oh shit," I said. The idea of my dad finding out made me feel sick.

"What's the worst they could do, anyway. Kick

you out of this godforsaken place? That would be a blessing." I shook my head, and J.B. found my hand and grasped it with his cold fingers.

"Hey, don't worry so much," he said, his voice dropping to a whisper as the lab door opened and Bruno returned from his break. "They won't get anything out of me. I'll play dead."

I smiled weakly, knowing he was just trying to cheer me up.

VII

J.B. was right. The very next morning, I was summoned to the Dean's office, called out of the physiology workshop by his secretary, who I followed meekly under the watchful eyes of my classmates. The office was spacious and elegantly furnished in dark walnut, but it felt crowded and oppressive when we entered. The Dean was seated behind a massive desk in the center of the room, flanked on either side with book shelves filled with bound medical journals. In front of the bookcases were four other men, sitting stiffly and looking grim. My advisor, an infectious disease expert I had only met once before, was on the left. Next to him, I recognized Dr. Anderson from our Intro to Psychiatry class. On the right side was the Assistant Dean, a jolly man in charge of student affairs who liked to regale the class with his med school exploits when he was supposed to be lecturing us on medical ethics. He had barely tried to conceal a chuckle when girlie slides appeared at his lecture. Beside him, looking stricken and insignificant, sat my father.

"That will be all, Agnes," the Dean said to his secretary as she ushered us in. "No disturbances please." Agnes shut the door and the Dean motioned to a folding chair placed immediately in front of his desk. "Caroline, please, have a seat."

I sat down warily, not daring to look at my father. It had never occurred to me that he might be called in. I was an adult, after all. What right had they to involve him?

"I don't know if you understand why you're here," the Dean began slowly, as though talking to a small child, "but I had a very disturbing phone call at the beginning of the week."

I took a deep breath, vowing to give away nothing.

The Dean peered at me closely. "Mrs. Marlene B. called to inform us that she received a visitor from the school last week. An unwelcome visitor."

They had figured out who I was in no time at all. All it took was a call to Yee, who told them where she'd left her ID. They had Marlene come in—she was only too happy to do so—and study a copy of the class picture where she quickly pointed me out. The Dean had interviewed her himself, emphasizing to me the gravity of the matter. He was an extremely busy person. I kept silent and did not try to deny any of it.

"There is more than one troubling aspect to this incident," the Dean said, clearing his throat. "I hardly need to emphasize the extreme inappropriateness of obtaining the file and visiting the family in the first place." He looked at me as though for concurrence, but I kept my expression in check. "It would appear that the widow's integrity in this matter, this highly sensitive matter of anatomic bequests, was called into question and she took great offense. In fact, it was a very unpleasant conversation."

It seemed I had not only wasted the Dean's time, but also subjected him to a brow-beating from Marlene. "Most disturbing of all is what Mrs. B. reported that you told her." Here the Dean exchanged looks with Dr. Anderson, the psychiatrist. "She claimed you told her you had been in communication with her deceased husband, that you were there at his request."

The room fell silent as they waited for my response. I knew I had to say something, but my throat was like parchment and I was perspiring uncomfortably.

"Couldn't she have misunderstood?" I finally managed to ask, my voice squeaky and dry. Out of the corner of my eye, I could see my father's face relax a little. Dr. Anderson cleared his throat, gave me a sympathetic smile, and then glanced at the Dean.

"If I may. Caroline, are you saying that you were not, somehow, in communication with the donor?"

"Do you mean with Marlene?" I asked.

"No," he said. His voice was slow and patient. "I mean with the deceased."

"With our cadaver?" I asked with as much incredulity as I could muster.

When I was younger, in those wilder years, I had managed to extricate myself from any number of scrapes with the simple technique of answering every question with a question of my own. "Do I look like I'm under twenty-one?" I might ask with feigned indignance to the bouncer at a club. "Are you claiming I had a boy spend the night?" I would ask the resident advisor at my college dorm who knocked timidly on my door in the morning while said boy snored softly under the flowered duvet covering my single bed. I did not like to flat-out lie, mainly because it did not seem to work. Lies were transparent. They showed in your face, in your voice. But questions were just questions. In this case, though, lying would seem like a betrayal of J.B. I could not bring myself to say I never conversed with him. At the time, he was my closest friend.

I found I did not have to, though. My father spoke up at this point with a question of his own.

"Are we to believe this woman over my daughter, John?" he asked the Dean, who shrugged uncomfortably. They asked me a few more questions about the visit to Marlene's and how I had obtained the file. I answered those truthfully enough. The interview drew to a close with some further admonishments and injunctions that seemed to have already been decided upon. I was to be scheduled for some individual sessions with Dr. Anderson. I was to be moved to a different cadaver table. I would not be permitted to attend the evening sessions, which wound up shortly afterward anyway for lack of attendees. I was never to contact Marlene again. Just as the meeting was coming to a close and everyone was rising from the chairs, I summoned my courage and asked another question.

"So, I was wondering," I said, my voice small and meek again. "About the policy for getting consent." My father gave me such an intense look that I had to avert my eyes, but I persevered. "I just wonder if it wouldn't be better for the actual person whose body is being donated to be the one who consents." The men looked at each other. "Before they die, I mean."

The Dean frowned. The Assistant Dean stepped forward as though he were accustomed to fending off these kinds of annoyances before they could reach the Dean. He patted my shoulder and nudged me gently towards the door.

"Caroline, it's a complicated question. We will certainly give it some thought." Then the meeting was over, and my father and I walked together slowly down the hallway.

That was one of the longest walks of my life. I did not know what to say to my father, and he said nothing until we reached the elevator alcove, where he would descend to the street to return to his clinic while I returned to my physiology lab three floors above. We pushed both the up and down buttons and waited in silence while the floors lit up one by one on the console above the elevator door. Finally, just as the elevator arrived, he turned to me, his face slumped and looking much older than moments before.

"I thought we had done with the shenanigans, Caroline," he said, shaking his head and stepping into the elevator before I could think of a reply.

VIII

I thought the worst of it was over then, but when I returned to school the following day I soon realized the whole class seemed to be aware of what had taken place. I had thought the meeting was supposed to be confidential, but someone, maybe Agnes, the secretary, or more likely the Assistant Dean, had found the charge against me too titillating to keep to themselves. In lecture hall, too many students had a sudden need to stretch and turn to the back of the room, stealing surreptitious glances at me to see whether I had grown antennae or fangs overnight. Maryellen Kearny, the unofficial class social director and a tireless gossip, made her way to my seat at the end of the lecture. She had never before so much as looked in my direction.

"If you ever need anything, Caroline," she said in her modulated voice, putting her carefully manicured hand over mine, "or just want to talk, I'm here. Okay?" I was horrified. Welch turned around and rolled his eyes as she left and then, always the gentleman, walked me out of the building before anyone else could offer their support.

"It'll blow over soon, Zach," he told me. "Believe me."

They went on to interview everyone around me. The Ws backed me up completely. No, they had not seen any untoward behavior. I was appropriate in class. Professional even. I was everything a medical student should be. They each told me this in turn after returning from their interviews. Bruno defended me as well. He could not exactly admit to leaving his post during those evening sessions, and I had admitted to sneaking into his files, absolving him of any blame. Even Dr. Nash took my side, saying I was a diligent student and improving steadily. It helped that I had aced the midterm, which took place shortly after my interview. Stenger whined about the hand gestures that were always blamed on him, but I don't think anyone took him seriously.

Carla Stein turned out to be my biggest ally. She stopped me outside the lecture hall to tell me about her interview where she, like everyone else, had supported me. Unlike others, she had no interest in salacious details about my role in the whole affair or rumors that I had had a psychotic break. Instead, she wanted to know more about the consent and what I had learned from the files.

"I heard you had a look at the files and that you thought your cadaver wasn't properly consented." I was happy that someone cared about the real issue and said yes, that was true.

"Did you happen to look at any of the others?"

As a matter of fact, I had. While I was looking at J.B.'s file, I managed to glance at a few others, curious about this very question. Stein's cadaver, E.W., the bald woman, had signed her own consent months before her death. Stein was relieved to hear this. But a number of others lying on the tables nearby us, had not. J.B.'s was not a unique case. Many of the consents were signed by spouses or children of the deceased.

"How can they do that?" Stein crossed her arms and shook her head. "It can't be right."

"I know," I said. "What if someone's just too cheap to pay for funeral expenses?"

Stein took notes on which cadavers had not been consented. She had been looking for a cause, I thought as I watched her walk off with her purposeful gait. This one was tailor-made. Over the next few months, she gathered hundreds of signatures from students and staff and petitioned the Medical Ethics Committee. She even contacted students from other medical schools to push the issue. Ultimately, the school had to change its policies. These days, all medical schools require written antemortem consent from the anatomical donor. I like to think that J.B. and I may have had a tiny influence on that.

Although I supported her, I did not attend Stein's

meetings or involve myself in any way with her activities. I thought it best to keep a low profile. I attended class, took notes, and studied harder than I ever had.

I was sent to Dr. Anderson as planned, but I believe I disappointed him. I'm sure he was hoping to find some interesting pathology, something reportable even that would result in a paper with a catchy title such as "Medical Student Exhibits Signs of Reverse Corpse Disorder." He was the type who cared more about his case files than his cases themselves. Our first visit was shortly after the Dean's meeting, and he seemed enthusiastic at first. He asked for a lot of background information about my family, my college days, and my sleep habits. He wanted to know how I got along with my father. He asked how old I was when my mother died but seemed to have no other interest in that. He sat back in his armchair, scratching with a pen on a clipboard chart. After several minutes he put down the clipboard and leaned forward on his seat.

"Tell me," he said, looking at me for the first time since I entered his office and rubbing his hands together, "a little bit about your relationship with J.B."

"Our cadaver?" I asked.

"Your cadaver," he confirmed. Did he think he would trip me up by sliding in the question in that manner, as though he were asking about another family member?

"I stand on the right side," I said, "or I stood on his right side when I was assigned to that table. I got to dissect the biliary tree."

"Hmmm," he said, tapping his pen on the clipboard. "How did that feel?"

"Kind of rubbery, actually," I said. "Almost like a chicken gizzard. The gallbladder was full of stones."

This was clearly not what he was looking for. He tried a different tack.

"How do you feel towards the cadaver as an individual, as a formerly living person, I mean?"

"How does anyone feel about someone who is dead?" I asked, thinking it was time to come up with a question. He didn't respond though, and waited for me to expand. "Wouldn't it depend entirely on your relationship when that person was alive? I mean how do you feel?" I asked him.

He smiled and said, "We're talking about you here, Caroline. What made you decide to break into the files and then visit the family?"

"'Break in' seems a little harsh," I told him. "The key was sitting right there." He could not be led into an argument about semantics, though, and continued waiting for me to speak. "I just, I don't know how," I finally said, "but I had a feeling that some of the cadavers, ours included, had not agreed to be there."

"This feeling," Dr. Anderson spoke slowly. "Did it arise from some communication from J.B., your cadaver?"

I shook my head, exasperated. "Look, I turned out to be right, didn't I? What does it matter how I knew it? The school, the department is wrong to be using cadavers of people who did not actually volunteer. We are supposed to advocate for our patients. That's all I was doing."

"So you feel your cadaver is like a patient. That you must care for him or her?"

"Our very first patient," I said. His eyebrows rose. "That's what Dr. Nash said the first day of class."

Over the course of the next few weeks, he grilled me over and over again. He could not get me to admit to any unhealthy obsession with our cadaver or anything else. No, I did not hear voices. No, I did not think anyone was out to get me. I knew exactly what was meant by "a stitch in time saves nine" and "do not put your eggs in one basket." When he pressed me more about J.B. and why I had gone to Marlene's, I just kept telling him that I was concerned there was not proper consent. Then I would turn the conversation to my mother. After a few sessions he grew bored and finally referred me to a therapist, a very nice lady, who did want to discuss my mother and who gave me a cassette tape of relaxation exercises that I listened to frequently for several years. To this day, whenever I cannot sleep, I will still conjure her scratchy voice telling me to tense and then relax my large toe. Then, my other toes. Then, my entire foot. And so on, and so forth, up my entire body. It is very soothing.

I tried my best to reassure my father, who seemed to have grown smaller and sadder when I visited him a few weeks later. I had not seen or spoken with him since the Dean's meeting until I rode the L to our house following midterms. It was Saint Patrick's Day and every year we made a corned beef and cabbage dinner. This had been my mother's custom, even though my father, who was Irish, had always eschewed the tradition as having nothing to do with Ireland. We had continued it after her death, although neither of us could cook. The end result might not have been palatable, but the odor of the simmering meat and spices—the aromatic woodiness of the cloves, the pungent sharpness of coriander—always summoned her back to us. We did not speak of the incident at school that day. We never spoke of it again. I reported my good midterm results and I know he was relieved about that. We sat in companionable silence, I with my Bates Introduction to Physical Examination and Dad with his journals, until it was time to chew our rubbery meat and swallow the tasteless cabbage. Then I allowed my father to drive me back to my apartment.

In cadaver lab, they moved me far away to be the fifth at a table that held an elderly man whose atrophied organs disintegrated at the slightest touch. This was a table of Ms who were guarded and unfriendly, not only to me, but also to each other. They acted as though they were still cut-throat pre-med students, carefully shielding their notes from each other. They did not welcome me there and I stood to the side much of the time, watching them work.

Yee returned to the class after midterms with no explanation of where she had been. She took her place at the table with the Ws and J.B. Marlene had convinced the school that J.B. was there of his own free will and his dissection continued, despite protests from Stein and her group. To do otherwise might have been admitting wrongdoing. I can see that now, but I still felt horrible about it. All I had wanted to do was to get him out of there, and now he had to endure his disassembly by himself, with no one at all to talk to. Yee was interested in the rumors concerning me and, unlike before, went out of her way to be friendly to me. Her first day back, she plopped herself down next to me in lecture hall rather than her usual seat and said, as though we had been great friends all along, "I hear you've been getting in trouble without me, Zachry."

"More like trying to stay out of trouble," I said, happy that she wanted to talk. She was not at all mad about the use of her ID, and told me, laughingly, she would leave it in the locker in case I needed it again. I was suspicious at first, but I was also flattered by her attention. We became friends of a sort, occasionally studying or having lunch together. In the beginning, she tried to get me to talk about J.B., but I was as tight-lipped with her as I was with Dr. Anderson. You could not trust anyone.

"So, what was the deal with you and the cadaver?" she asked the first time we went to lunch together and had a table to ourselves in the cafeteria.

"What's the deal with you missing the beginning of the semester?" I countered.

"I don't know," she said, looking at me evenly. "I just wasn't into it. The whole med school thing."

"Well, I just wasn't into it either," I said. "The whole lack-of-consent thing." She grinned and let it go after that. Later she explained to me that her parents were very strict and it had always been expected that she would go to medical school. She had dreamed of art school at one point, but that was not even a possibility for her parents. Towards the end of the winter break, she had developed a severe case of shingles, from stress, her physician had told her.

"You never look the least bit stressed," I said. "Everything seems so easy for you."

"That's just my persona, Zachry. I work hard, like everyone else."

She had milked the shingles as long as she could, claiming severe pain and fatigue, hoping that if she lost enough time she would not be able to return that semester, and possibly her parents would just let it go. But she was getting bored, she realized, at home with her parents. She didn't think she could win them over so she might as well just return and make the best of it.

"That's what we both need to do," she told me. "Just make the best of it."

It turned out she did work hard. We spent a lot of time in the library together. Yee was very focused on studying for boards, although she did complain a lot about how boring it all was. I, on the other hand, though I would never admit it to her, found myself getting more interested in my studies. Instead of just memorizing muscles and bones, we were now deep into our physiology class and learning clinical correlations. We had started an introductory course on history-taking and physical exam, and I wished I'd been able to do one with J.B., although I might not have been able to get him to stop joking long enough to take it seriously. I began thinking that my father had been right, that this would be a good path for me, and I was already looking forward to second year, when there would be interaction with real patients. I had no particular talents but believed that had I had an inclination to something less secure, say music or the arts, my father would have supported me in that pursuit. He would have been thrilled to see me work hard at anything after my less-than-steady college career. I felt badly for Yee and her need to comply with her family's demands despite her obvious artistic talent. So I feigned disinterest and aloofness to the whole enterprise along with her and listened to her rhapsodize about new exhibits at the Art Institute and her plans to one day travel to Florence.

The only thing we really had in common was a feeling that we were outsiders, not typical medical students, perhaps not really supposed to be there. That was silly, in retrospect, since both of our fathers were physicians. But now I had an excuse to wander over to J.B.'s table, ostensibly to visit with Yee and the Ws. The Ws liked to include me, and Wilson would always give me a tour of their progress, quizzing me on the more obscure nerves and blood vessels. Bruno would look up and frown when he saw me over there. I think he had been given instructions to watch me closely and keep me away from J.B., but there was really nothing he could do. The after-hours lab was shut down, unlikely to ever re-open, and he had me to thank for that.

IX

After some time had passed, I felt I had to try to speak with J.B. at least once more. They were taking him apart bit by bit and soon there would be nothing at all left of him. Of course, I could not attempt it during our lab sessions when he was surrounded by my lab mates and the other students were milling nearby. The lab was never left unlocked now. My locker was in the adjacent hall which gave me the excuse to walk by frequently, and if no one was there, I would try the door. One day I saw Wilson coming out of the lab and turning a key carefully in the door behind him. He turned in time to see me casually putting on the jacket and slinging on the backpack I had just retrieved from my locker.

"Oh, hey Wilson," I said.

"Zachry," he nodded. "You haven't seen McMann around, have you?"

I shook my head. McMann was a friend of Welch's and, like Yee, had disappeared for several weeks after winter break. He was now back, trying to make up for lost time. Unlike Yee, he had returned with a clear explanation, mononucleosis, and had the weight loss and sallow cheeks to prove it. Wilson was tutoring him in the lab, I learned. And Wilson had a key.

"A no-show, I guess," Wilson said and walked with me to the elevator and then out the door. We walked together for a little bit, talking, and I learned that Wilson tutored several students on Friday afternoons and then took the L home to the apartment on the South Side he shared with his wife. She was expecting their first child, he said, and had severe hyperemesis gravidarum. He looked at me to ascertain whether I knew the medical term for morning sickness and went on when I nodded sympathetically. She got so bad he had taken her to the ER for IV rehydration a couple of times.

"Gosh," I said. "I didn't know it could be that bad." Wilson had never been so forthcoming. I could tell he was worried. He walked quickly with his long legs, and I had to scamper to keep up with him. After a couple of blocks, he turned west towards the L station, and I turned east towards my apartment building. When we parted, I had hatched a plan.

The following Friday, I lingered for quite some time between my locker and the lab door, walking purposefully in one direction or the other or rummaging through the locker whenever someone walked by. When the lab door finally opened and I saw Wilson and McMann emerge, I stood back in another door-way until I was sure Wilson was headed home. Then I followed him.

When he was almost at the station, I had to run to catch up with him and got there just as he reached the stairs.

"Wilson!" I called just as he started his ascent. He looked over.

"You headed to the South Side, Zach?" he asked, one eyebrow raised.

"My keys!" I said, panting. "I'm pretty sure I left my keys in the cadaver lab. I need them to get into my apartment."

I had left a set of keys in the lab that afternoon, but they were the keys to my dad's house, not my apartment keys. I didn't want to be locked out if the plan failed.

"I thought," I said, hesitating, "that you might have keys. I looked around for Bruno but he doesn't seem to be there." Bruno always left early on Fridays; I had learned this during my reconnaissance over the previous weeks.

Wilson sighed, looked up towards the station en-trance, and then at his watch. The rumble of a train could be heard in the distance. He seemed to vacillate, and I was afraid for a minute he would walk back with me to the lab. But he reached into his pocket and handed me the keys.

"Give them back Monday," he said, and then turned to bound up the stairs. He stopped halfway and called back to me.

"Zachry. Please don't get me into trouble."

Did I feel guilty, taking advantage of the fact that Wilson's wife was sick in order to get the keys from him? I know I did. But I didn't give a second thought to what would happen if it was discovered that he had loaned me the keys to the lab. I probably assumed that he would be afforded the same kind of immunity that I had been given for my offense: a stern warning from the Dean and a slight reduction of privileges.

When I reached the lab, I opened the lid to J.B.'s table gingerly, half afraid that there would be nothing there. I had seen what they were doing to his face already when I would visit the lab table. But there he was, waiting for me, his right hand twitching, his remaining eye staring right at me. The left eye had been pulled out of its socket to examine the optic nerve and vessels that lay behind it. It lay useless on his temple.

"Kiddo," I heard him say although it sounded more like "iddo." His voice was barely audible.

"J.B. How are you?" A stupid question, but I wanted to sound cheerful. I held his hand which was cold and limp, but he managed to tap mine with his fifth finger, the only one that had not been dissected. He grunted and said something else that I could not make out at all. Then there was quiet, and I tried to fill in the space by telling him everything that had happened. I told him about Dr. Anderson, the psychiatrist, how he found me so boring. He made little snorting sounds at that and I think he was trying to say, "head shrinks." He probably knew some great jokes involving psychiatrists and I wished I could make out what he was saying. I told him about my improved grades, the upcoming board examinations about which I and most the class were terrified. I told him all about Stein's petition and the end result. I didn't need to tell him that it had made no difference for him or any of the other cadavers whose families had consented on their behalf. Here he still was, more mutilated than ever. I jabbered on like this for a while and then fell silent. Ours had always been a two-way relationship. I could not carry on the conversation by myself. The room was eerily quiet. Without the hum of the fluorescent lights, the buzzing of other students, or Bruno's radio playing in the corner, it felt cold and tomb-like. My breathing was the only sound. Finally, J.B. made another attempt to speak.

"Ohh," he said in a drawn-out way. I waited for more, but he tapped my hand and repeated it. "Ohh," he said again.

"J.B.? I'm sorry, I don't know what you're saying."

"Ohh," he said the third time, and I finally got it.

"Smoke, you want a smoke!" His eye seemed to glimmer then and I knew I had heard right. But my face fell. I had given them up completely a few weeks ago, inspired by the thoracic cavity dissection. It had been a struggle but I had done it.

"J.B., I'm so sorry. I don't have any. I quit! I threw them all out. I should have saved one for you." I was so angry with myself that I had not anticipated the one little thing I might do for him. "I'll run out and get a pack. It won't take long." He was so completely still now; I could barely detect any life in the eye, but I felt a slight motion in the finger again and I told him I would be back soon. "Don't worry," I told him.

Closing the lid softly, I picked up my backpack and turned toward the door to leave. I was startled to see a figure standing there watching me. Bruno.

I was so surprised, I said nothing at first, but then I remembered my excuse. The keys should still be there, on the counter behind a book on the opposite side of the room where I had hidden them earlier in the day.

"My keys," I said, walking over to the counter and grabbing them. I held them up for Bruno to see.

"I forgot my apartment keys," I said, my voice breathless. "The door was unlocked." The deception seemed so obvious that I thought my words might freeze in the air and shatter on the linoleum floor.

Bruno walked over, looked at my hand, then held his out to me. I was confused at first, not understanding what he wanted until I saw, with horror, that I was holding both sets of keys: the house keys and the lab keys. I handed over the lab keys.

"Where'd you get these, miss?" he asked, but did not wait for my response. "That boy gave these to you, didn't he?" I knew that by "that boy" he meant Wilson, but I was caught off guard by the way he spit it out, by the anger in his voice.

"Bruno," I said, "we thought you'd left and I was locked out of my apartment. Wilson had to get home to his wife. She's sick." Bruno just shook his head, looking at the keys.

"They never gave keys to a student before," he said. "Always just Bruno and the professors. First there's the cabinet and they say 'Bruno, why are the cabinets not secure?' I say 'Sorry, I thought I can trust.'" Here he gave me a pointed look and I glanced down. I didn't know he had been blamed for my getting into the files. "Then they give the key to this, this," he paused and finally spat out, "student. And I ask 'why now?' I ask 'why, after fifteen years give keys to a student? Why after what happen with the young miss?'" He nodded in my direction. "They say students is struggling and I say 'Bruno can help them.' But no, Bruno don't have the degree, Bruno only work here fifteen years, Bruno only take blame when things go wrong."

I had no idea he had been nursing this grievance against Wilson, against me. He seemed his same old self during lab hours, humming along as he wandered the tables. I wondered now if he only pretended to leave early on Fridays, circling back to make sure things were locked up, to check up on Wilson.

"Bruno," I said, pleading with him, "no one has to know. Wilson was just trying to help me get home. I was going to give him back the keys on Monday." I held out my hand, but I knew that was useless.

"No, miss. Not on your life." He shook his head and pocketed the keys. "I report on everything. Dr. Nash asked me. The young miss we watch. Even you cost me my job, I report it." He walked to the door and held it open for me and I knew there was no use in arguing further. He wanted to show Dr. Nash that Wilson had been a mistake. That he'd been wrong to trust anyone but Bruno with the keys. I walked out slowly, glancing back at J.B.'s table before Bruno shut and locked the door. There would be no last smoke now. Bruno waited for me to walk to the elevator, ignoring the tears that were spilling onto my face. He even got onto the elevator with me and punched the button for the ground floor to make sure I was leaving. Then he stepped out and held the door for a second. "Miss, about that number thirty." He jerked his head back towards the lab. "You gotta let that go."

In the lobby, I stood and watched as water droplets snaked down the plate glass from a spring drizzle. I had no idea what to do. If I was expelled from school, my father would be devastated. I couldn't even begin to think of what it would mean if Wilson was. As I stood there, wiping my face with the back of my hand, Welch came out of the stairwell, fiddling with an umbrella. "Night, Zachry." Then he stopped and looked back at me.

"Caroline? What is it?" It must have been obvious I'd been crying. I shook my head, fighting back a new onslaught of tears. After a second, I managed to cough out an explanation of how I had borrowed Wilson's keys and got caught in the lab by Bruno.

"Yikes," said Welch, who knew, as did the whole class, that I was under special scrutiny. He may have known what it could mean to Wilson as well.

"I don't care about me," I said, "but it'll kill my dad if I get kicked out.

"I don't think they'd do that," Welch said slowly.

"But what about Wilson?" I asked.

"He was just trying to help you out, Caroline. But he shouldn't have given you the keys."

"He needed to get home to his wife," I said. "She's been sick."

"She has?" he asked. "Still, he was kind of pushing it to even invite you over to our table. He should have been more careful. But I don't think anyone will blame you."

This was worse than anything I expected. If Welch only knew how devious I had been, waiting until Wilson was nearly on the train home.

"He was really worried about his wife, though," I said in almost a whisper. If I could not convince even Welch, I was not sure what I'd do. We stood there for a minute, not saying anything, and then Welch patted me on the shoulder and offered me the umbrella.

"Take it, he said, "I've got to go back upstairs. I just remembered something." I refused the umbrella, and after he left, I walked out into the now heavy downpour. I was hoping to get soaked through, hoping it might trigger some illness, a cold that would become a pneumonia, just like in a Jane Austen novel. But we had been taught otherwise and I remained as healthy as ever.

X

I stayed in my apartment all weekend, not even bothering to go out for groceries. I spent the time studying, although I asked myself what the point was. I
doubted I would be allowed to sit for exams. On Monday, I left early, hoping to catch Wilson before he met
with anyone else. The least I could do would be to
warn him. The storm had cleared over the weekend,
and the air was soft with the scent of spring. Trees
had budded out into baby greens, and a few tulips
bloomed along the parkway of my block, a sign of the
gentrification soon to come to the neighborhood. A
group of students mingled outside our building, re-
luctant to go inside on such a fine day. I walked by
them unnoticed and realized that the stares and whispered conversations left in my wake had dwindled to

nothing in the previous few weeks. I fumbled at my locker for a few minutes, thinking of what I would say to Wilson and where to look for him. When I looked up, he was striding down the hall towards me.

"Zachry," he said before reaching me. "I'm so sorry. I shouldn't have left you stranded like that. You get home okay?" His look of concern was difficult to bear.

"I did." I started to say more but he kept talking.

"I've been so worried about my wife. Her weight was down fifteen pounds at her prenatal visit last week and I can barely keep her hydrated."

"I'm sorry, Wilson," I said but he interrupted again.

"But I should have helped you find your keys. Anyway, she's a little better today and you got home. Can I get my lab keys?"

"I don't have them," I said slowly looking up at him with a pained expression. "Bruno took them." Wilson's face changed instantly and he stared at me in disbelief.

"Bruno was there? I was sure he'd already left."

"He came in while I was looking for my keys," I said, "and he was pretty upset. He said he was going to talk to Nash."

Wilson sighed and closed his eyes for a moment. "I should have gone with you," he said when he opened them. Then he looked at me and said, "Don't worry, Zach, it's not your fault. You had to get home. I'll go talk to Nash." He headed towards the office and I felt worse than ever. I knew I should go with him right then and confess everything to both of them. How it had been a ruse, how it was not Wilson's fault at all. But I felt paralyzed. I went to the library instead and tried to study. Lectures started at nine, and I made my way there a few minutes after the hour, dreading another encounter with Wilson.

He was standing there outside the doors, waiting for me. His anger was obvious even before I got close enough to see his face: his posture rigid, his arms folded over his chest. Every muscle of his face was tense and his eyes were like sharp crystals. He looked angrier than I'd ever seen him.

"What happened?" I asked in a loud whisper; the lecture had already started inside. He did not answer me directly. "You know, Zachry," he said in a low and seething voice, "I don't have the kind of daddy that can come down here and get me out of scrapes like you do." That stung, the more so because it was true. "And even if he had that kind of clout, my daddy wouldn't do it. He bailed me out once when I was young, a teenager. He said that would be the one time and he stuck to it." He paused; his look had not softened at all. A couple of late students rushed past us to enter the lecture hall. They stared at us as they entered the hall, shutting the door softly behind them.

"Wilson," I said, "I'm really sorry."

"Bruno said you had our table open in there. Number thirty. He told Nash I'd been encouraging you. Did you even actually lose your keys?"

I started to speak, but he interrupted. "I don't want to hear it. I don't even want to know. Just don't involve me anymore."

"Okay," I said, trying to keep my voice even.

"I mean it," he said. "Just stay away." I nodded and turned to go. I could not face lecture now. "Oh, and Zachry," Wilson said, his voice as harsh as ever, "Nash wants to see you in his office before lab starts."

Nash looked weary when I knocked on his door, and he gestured to a seat in front of his desk. It was my first time inside his office, and I was struck by its austerity. The books on the shelves were sparse and interspersed with few objects: a porcelain vase, an abstract sculpture, a framed photograph of a jagged, snow-topped mountain. Everything looked precisely and deliberately placed, without a stray piece of paper or pen in sight. His desk was a simple table, completely bare except for his pointing stick, which he gripped tightly as I sat down in front of him.

"You know, Caroline," he began after an uncomfortable silence, "everyone has gone out of their way for you more than once now." I nodded in acknowledgment, waiting to let him say his piece before I jumped in to plead for Wilson. "We trusted you to respect the boundaries that were set regarding table thirty." No one referred to J.B. by his name or initials. It was always table thirty. "I trusted you. Wilson trusted you. Even Bruno, though he may have harbored some doubts, did not expect to find you leaning over table thirty the way he did the other night." J.B. trusted me, too, I wanted to tell him. J.B. trusted me to help him and I had failed utterly. He paused and rolled the pointing stick under his hands a few times.

"So, I'm at a loss now. A complete loss."

"I just want to say," I started to tell him, "that Wilson was only trying to—"

"We're not talking about Wilson here. I know all about Wilson. We're talking about you."

It seemed he did not want to report to the Dean but made me promise not to go near table thirty ever again. I was not to "even look in that direction," he said, or talk with my former lab mates during lab or do anything but enter the lab during class, proceed straight to table eighteen where I was currently assigned, and then exit the lab directly when class was finished. I nodded when he asked if I understood, amazed that I was getting off this easy. "But what about Wilson?" I blurted out as he was standing up to dismiss me. "What about his tutoring job and his keys?"

"That's over and done with, Caroline," he said as he crossed the room and opened the door, indicating it was time for me to go. "But you should know that you, at least, have some pretty good friends here."

I was not sure what he meant by that until I learned that Welch had intervened on both Wilson's and my behalf, probably the very same night I went into the lab. Welch and Nash were friends for reasons I never understood. They had some past history. Wilson, too, had stood up for me when he spoke to Nash, which astounded me, angry as he'd been. I learned all this from Welch a few days later when he explained that the tutoring job was really just about over, anyway, and that Nash had to appease Bruno in some way. We were standing in the hallway outside the library, the sun streaming in the large windows that faced the hospital looming over us from across the street. Welch's dark hair was lit up with a whitish glow, and I could picture him, years in the future, standing in that hospital, with that same tilt of his head and sympathetic smile, comforting some patient or family member. I realized by then he had no interest in me beyond friendship, but I wanted badly to deserve that friendship.

In the few remaining weeks of lab, I followed the restrictions as closely as I could. Bruno watched me constantly, and his humming would cease or turn into a low growl whenever he came near me. Wilson was still very angry with me and would not even look in my direction. Yee, on the other hand, made faces at me, trying to get me to laugh, and Welch would give me encouraging smiles whenever he was near. Weiss continued to share his notes with me, always considering me to be part of the "table thirty team," as he called us. I don't know if he was even aware of what had happened. Once, he tracked me down with a plastic bag full of homemade peanut butter cookies. "Study aids from Marjorie," he said. "She didn't want me to eat them all."

That Friday night excursion into the lab was the last time I spoke with J.B. He was never the same. Now he was just a cadaver, like the others. A deflated, lifeless shell. There was only one time that I thought I glimpsed a flicker of the old J.B. again. We had continued with the face and neck dissections, and I had given up any hope of ever speaking to him again. How could he speak with his mouth pulled apart like that, his tongue released from the root? But I would steal glances at him whenever I entered or left the lab, hoping for something. I was leaving early on one of our final afternoon sessions while the Ws and Yee were still working. They had J.B.'s head positioned way to the side as they pulled out the sternocleidomastoid and searched for vessels with their teasing needles. His face was pointed towards me and I saw him, just for a brief moment, open his eye and stare right at me. The rest of his face was a mess, so it was impossible to know what his expression might have been. But I smiled sadly at him and mouthed, "I'm sorry, J.B." He closed his eye for the final time.

At the end of the semester, a few weeks before we broke for summer, a multi-denominational service was held for our cadavers. This was a first at our school, although I understand it is now commonplace. Stein had pushed for this, although I don't think she was at all religious. We were busy studying for our first board exams, so I was surprised by how packed the auditorium was for this optional event. Even Stenger was there. I had been given to understand that it might be best if I did not attend. Dr. Nash had stopped me after class the day previously, looking uncomfortable, and said that the Dean's office wanted me to know that I was not expected or required to attend. I had not been planning to up to that moment. But I faced him, hands on my hips, and asked, "So, I'm not allowed there?"

He looked abashed and said, "No, I don't think that's what was meant at all. I think they just meant, if you're not comfortable, if it's at all difficult for you, it might not be necessary." He struggled to finish the sentence.

"I'll take that into consideration," I said, turning to go.

"Zachry," he said, calling after me. "As far as I'm concerned you can go or not. You're a decent student." By that, I think he meant I was a decent person, which was one and the same thing in his estimation. But he had no idea.

I went to the service, arriving at the last minute and hoping to get a seat in the back. But the moment I arrived, all four of my former lab partners, Yee, Welch, Weiss, and Wilson, were seated together, and Yee and Welch turned around and waved me over. They had saved me a seat.

"You're still one of us," Weiss said in his monotone voice when I sat down. "There's no escaping it." Wilson gave me a brief nod as we waited for the program to begin. Then, reconsidering, he leaned over and whispered that he thought he would get his tutoring job back again in the fall if there was a need. I sighed with relief and asked him how his wife was doing.

"She's better," he said. "She's good actually, now that she's hit second trimester. I think we're gonna make it." He smiled broadly at me, his face looking more relaxed than I'd ever seen it. I felt I had been forgiven, though I did not feel I deserved it. Wilson and his wife had a healthy baby boy the following fall, and I think they had several more kids after that. He would later join his father and brother in their South Side general surgery practice and then go on to do a colorectal specialty and join the staff at County and Lake Park. I saw him occasionally at conferences and sent him a few patients over the years, telling them he was the best colon cancer surgeon in town, which was true. Most of my patients, I found, did not want to travel to that part of town.

During the service for our cadavers, a hospital chaplain and rabbi presented some prayers and gave brief sermons about sacrifice and the ever after. There was a vocal soloist, a hospital volunteer who was a semi-professional contralto and sang "Amazing Grace." Then they read the names of the deceased, and if the family had provided one, they projected photographs. When J.B.'s appeared on the screen, I was taken off guard. I had assumed Marlene would have wanted nothing to do with this. The image was a faded and overexposed snapshot taken at night in a backyard somewhere. There was a younger J.B. with his arm around Marlene, their pupils red from the camera flash. Marlene was looking off to the left, but J.B. looked straight at the camera, gesturing with a lit cigarette. He seemed to be saying something to the photographer, making a joke. I was startled to see this and more startled to feel my eyes welling up and a constriction forming in my throat. I felt Welch, sitting next to me, touch my hand very lightly. I looked his way with a thin smile, embarrassed by my emotion, and was surprised to see his eyes were shining, looking up at the screen. Welch would be dead within a decade, one of so many young men to perish during those early years of the AIDS epidemic when all that could be done was prayer, hand-wringing, and massive doses of anti-bacterial or anti-fungal antibiotics. I would attend his funeral and meet Wilson, Weiss, and Carla Stein, and the four of us would reminisce awkwardly. I would feel stupid for not realizing Welch was gay or that he had been in a relationship with Dr. Nash, chagrined by my crush on him. I would remember my brief, sunlit vision of Welch as an older physician and think that the world had suffered a terrible loss.

At the memorial for our cadavers, all four of my partners, even Yee, normally such a cynic, appeared moved by the ceremony, as did many others in the room. I was still embarrassed by my reaction. Thankfully, I was at the end of a row and managed to slip out to the back of the room without the rest of the class noticing.

Yee found me a short time later at our locker and handed me a rolled-up drawing she had made.

"Something to remember us by," she said. By us, I believe she meant both her and J.B. I unrolled it slowly and took a sharp breath when I saw it.

"I don't know what to say," I told her, studying the drawing. "It is so beautiful. And accurate. This is what you should be doing."

Yee nodded. "Yeah, I've been thinking about that."

She did not return to medical school the following fall, and that may have been the last time we ever spoke. A few years later, I learned she had become a medical illustrator, eventually quite well-known in her field. I still see her work in my medical journals from time to time. We did not stay in touch.

XI

The drawing. I am holding it in front of me now. It is what has led me back to that time after so many years. I found it in a box in my father's study, marked "Caroline - Med School" in my father's precise hand, once strong and confident, but here already diminishing and cramping into the telltale micrographia of Parkinsonism. I think I might more accurately date the multiple documents I have been going through by the condition of his handwriting as by any actual dates attached to them. I am amazed by the volume of stuff, the quantity of relics he has held onto. The drawing's edge was peeking out from my old Clemente's atlas with its broken spine and loosened pages, pressed between the sections on thorax and abdomen.

My father has finally passed, officially, out of this world. It seems to me he has been leaving it, little by little, for many years now. His departure began with my mother's illness and his resignation from the chief of staff position, abandoning his ambition for higher medical school roles. It continued through my youthful transgressions, each of which seemed to take an almost mortal bite out of him. Life steadied for a while after that. He found satisfaction in having me join him in his oncology practice for those few years before his retirement. Then Parkinson's began to afflict him, probably beginning much earlier than he or I realized if the progression of his handwriting is any indication. It took his strength and balance first, which was distressing but livable for a man of books and letters. When his mind started to go, when he lost his train of thought mid-sentence and could not recall the names of patients he had followed for years, he recoiled and withdrew in horror. His deterioration was rapid after that.

What's left of him now are his ashes, sitting in an unassuming cardboard canister on the dining room table, and this house. The house is to be sold, put on the market as soon as it is cleaned out. I told the realtor I wanted to do it myself: the sorting, the boxing up of items to be given away, the bagging of things to be tossed. One day into it I already know that I will abandon the project and call in the estate agent after all, allowing them to coldly assess each item for value, filling a dumpster with the sum of my parents' lives, of my childhood. This house is a sad shrine to the few happy years we spent here as a family. I find it hard to be here, to breathe the air in here which is so heavy with memory and nostalgia. The odors of my mother's cooking and the mustiness of my father's journals in the library still cling to the walls. It never felt this way while my father was still living, however nominally.

The drawing is in good condition. The paper has not yellowed and only one edge is frayed. The ink is still strong and the features richly detailed. J.B. is depicted from the shoulders up, his mouth gaping slightly, and that comical half-closed right eye gazing up at the viewer just as I remember it. When I look closely, amid the lines and cross hatches, I can see that the neck has already been opened, revealing the internal carotid and jugular. The cheek has also been interrupted, the parotid gland peeking out from behind the thin curls of peeled-back skin and with it the buccal branches of the facial nerve, delicately teased away from subcutaneous tissue.

The dissection of the face and neck is just beginning but he is still mainly intact, blissfully unaware of what is about to happen to him. He will be disassembled, peeled away layer by layer. His features will be removed—the eyeball, the tongue, the external ear—and carefully placed next to him or inside a cavity, like holiday poultry, no part wasted. Later, when we are done with him, all the parts will be bagged up carefully and removed to the mortuary to be cremated or buried with the whole. All that will be left will be a faded snapshot or a drawing, yellowing or gathering dust, in someone's closet.

It is the eye, though, that is the most remarkable feature of this drawing. Even with the lid half closed, the pupil cloudy and fixed, there is a brightness to it that cannot be ascribed only to my memory. There is a sharpness, a sentience there, and I think Yee must have seen it as well. I will study this drawing for a long time before I realize the light has faded and I need to get on with my task. I will place it carefully back in the pages of the atlas, along with a few important documents I have gathered to take with me. I will finger, regretfully, a few more items I have considered, a silver pendant necklace of my mother's, a worn book of poetry of my father's, before setting them back down and leaving the house for the final time. They will be abandoned with everything else. In the car, Clemente's on the seat next to me, I will open the book to look once more. J.B. will still be there. He will be looking right at me.

About Etchings Press

Etchings Press is a student-run publisher at the University of Indianapolis that runs a post-publication award—the Whirling Prize—as well as an annual publication contest for one poetry chapbook, one prose chapbook, and one novella. On occasion, Etchings Press publishes new chapbooks from previous winners. For more information about these contests and the Whirling Prize post-publication award, please visit etchings.uindy.edu.

Poetry
2023: *Other Side of Sea* by Xiaoqiu Qiu
2022: *A Place That Knows You*
   by Tiwaladeoluwa Adekunle
2022: *The Vaudeville Horse*
   by Elizabeth Kerlikowske
2021: *My Mother's Ghost Scrubs the Floor at 2 a.m.*
   by Robert Okaji
2020: *Vaginas Need Air* by Tori Grant Welhouse
2019: *As Lovers Always Do* by Marne Wilson
2018: *In the Herald of Improbable Misfortunes*
   by Robert Campbell
2017: *Uncle Harold's Maxwell House Haggadah*
   by Danny Caine
2016: *Some Animals* by Kelli Allen
2015: *Velocity of Slugs* by Joey Connelly
2014: Action at a Distance
   by Christopher Petruccelli

Prose
2023: *Leaving the House Unlocked*
   by Elizabeth Enochs (nonfiction)
2022: *Triple Point* by Laura Story Johnson (essays)
2021: Bad Man Love Stories
   by Curtis VanDonkelaar (fiction)
2020: *Three in the Morning and You Don't Smoke
   Anymore* by Peter J. Stavros (fiction)
2019: *Dissenting Opinion from the Committee for
   the Beatitudes* by Marc J. Sheehan (fiction)
2018: *The Forsaken* by Chad V. Broughman (fiction)
2017: *Unravelings*
   by Sarah Cheshire (memoir)
2016: *Pathetic* by Shannon McLeod (essays)
2015: *Ologies* by Chelsea Biondolillo (essays)
2014: *Static: Stories* by Frederick Pelzer (fiction)

Novella
2023: *Our Cadaver* by Elizabeth Toman
2022: *Goodbye to the Ocean* by Susan L. Lin
2021: *Miss Alma May Learns to Fight* by Stuart Rose
2020: *Under Black Leaves* by Doug Ramspeck
2019: *Savonne, Not Vonny* by Robin Lee Lovelace
2018: *Edge of the Known Bus Line*
   by James R. Gapinski
2017: *The Denialist's Almanac of American Plague
   and Pestilence* by Christopher Mohar
2016: *Followers* by Adam Fleming Petty

Chapbooks from Previous Winners
2022: *slighted...* by Chad V. Broughman (fiction)
2020: *Fruit Rot* by James R. Gapinski (fiction)
2016: *#LOVESONG*
   by Chelsea Biondolillo (microessays with photos
   and found text)

Colophon

Body text is Sitka Text
Cover Text is Californian FB

About the Author

Elizabeth Toman writes short fiction and creative nonfiction. Her work has appeared in *CALYX*, *Halfway Down the Stairs*, *Emerge*, and elsewhere. She works as a primary care physician in New Mexico.